Winter Fragments

Anthony Furlong

Autumn now and then

Febrile and frowzy
as squirrels munch on conkers
cygnets beat their wings

mist through cobwebs drip
like rimy dandelion moons
splosh squelch rustle slip

lonesome vintage scenes
freshly tinted rusty bronze
acorns minor keys

a sonorous crunch
of toe knee chest nut ambles
with in cheery fugue

Well the memory; flanked by tall hedgerows scattered red with
haws and hips

broken with gnarled pollards;

bent oak limbs in the still grey sky

betwixt meanders sinister the cobbled twin track of a narrow
empty lane;

listen to the scraping of my own footfall and the cries of corvids,

the smell of wood smoke

from a farmhouse built of mellowed Cheshire brick;

a gaggle of geese gabble amongst themselves,

the flaked paint sign reads FRESH EGGS For SALE

lifting the sneck the gate scrapes open

memory; on a whim the stripling nears a window

his peaked cap prods the glass

briefly seeing his own youthful reflection

within the blink of an eye he notices

an auld man sitting

besides a fire in quiet reverie;

turning away he stumbles on some persiflage

glancing up he spots

the fecund crimson breast of a Bullfinch

perched high upon a plum tree thicket

proud midst the pewter porringer sky

the aged peers out of his own window

and watches the whipper-snapper fade

into the winter distant

Harvesting filberts in the spring.

Somnolently passing through my secondary comprehensive education, more often than not gazing out of the class room windows. Currently observing the window cleaner and his deft use of a squeegee. Humming to my-self along to Oliver's Army or even Dexys – Geno Geno. Whilst paying scant regard to my pubescent contemporaries - but the teachers leery! Therefore to commence with a cliché – kids these days! I'm sitting at the back of the classroom, head down reciting a passage from Lorna Doon and feeling confident with this late afternoons lesson. Then finish reading to look up at the teacher blithely smiling, his chair reclining with hands clasped behind his head, his elbows akimbo, whilst puffing on his pipe. His chair then moves forwards creating its familiar creaking sound on its way, just before the bell rings signifying home time. Suddenly! All the children's desks open in synchronised agreement, books flung within before the lids slam shut! Home time, a change of clothes and out to play – childhood's expletives…

Surly it was Spring or maybe it was Autumn. I could have been aged seven or possibly about nine. When our geography teacher was explaining to our year that we will be going to this strange sounding place. There was of course a fee payable by our parents. I recall £15 but with concessions reducing the total amount. I listened intently. Other children with older siblings understood more than I. And were familiar with this peculiar sounding place described by the teacher. They appeared exited by the prospect. Then relevant written details were provided before being dismissed. Outside in the corridor voices were raised. Amongst this din I made enquiries to the usual 'clued up' kids – what's this place called again? Colla what? They laugh. Possibly teasing, boasting and exaggerating. Telling me of this place with its mountain. The name of which as yet I couldn't quite get a handle on. I walked home as per usual dawdling, scuffing my shoes, picking the leaves off privets. Preoccupied with another school note stuffed within my short trouser pocket. I can just about recall arriving home, observing their faces as the note was studied. A little apprehensive, I awaited their response.

Al last my bags were packed, my parked zipped right up - pinching my chin (all on my behalf). My Dad then breaks the rules by hiding 50p pieces in each one of my coat pockets, before I'm taken to the departure point. Then we board a big red bus or was it a green Crossville? I take a seat at the bottom of the spiral stair case ascending to the upper deck. Sitting quietly next to a fellow classmate we hear rowdiness from the upper deck. Returning apprehensive glances as the heavy grumbling of the vehicles engine begins. Signifying that we are about to set off. Then I look out of the window to be waved on our ways. Further were cheers from the upper deck!

The journey takes us to the city centre. Then along and through the Mersey tunnel. Possibly a little nervous, unsure; maybe now I'm being sentimental. But the the couple of kids I found myself sitting besides, I had never really bothered with prior to this. One of them was clever and always sat at the front of the class to the left of the teacher. Always neatly dressed in his grey V-neck jumper; probably purchased from George Henry Lees. The other kid was scruffy. After a little while we relaxed and started to chat. Distracting us from the long mysterious passage under the river and eventually out into daylight, then further on to be amongst the green rolling countryside. Today this very same trip doesn't seem like an expedition, but merely a drive.

Eventually the chugging slowed as the bus driver crunched down the gears and with considerable animated effort succeeded in turning the huge steering wheel sharply, as we enter this puzzling place known as Colla something. The bus cautiously proceeds along the tree lined drive and halts outside a cluster of these long wooden dormitories. We all alighted and stood patiently as the geography, the history teacher and the teacher who for ever was smoking his pipe, arranged us all into orderly lines. The air was crisp and fresh with the clean fragrance of lush vegetation. As we waited receiving instructions, verily I stood at the end of the line, allotting more attention to the scenery, and taking particular note of the numerous house martins and diligent sparrows.

That very same evening we slumbered in our earmarked bunk beds. Within these long dormitories we all awakened bright and breezy, before heading off for breakfast. Cold goats milk with cornflakes! Over the next few days we were galvanised, traipsing and tramping about the mountains foothills – Moel Famau shrouded in dense mist and dread. Like Mount Kinabalu, Monodnock or even Katahdin! On one such walk we all followed the river – Affon Alyn to the Devils gorge! Likewise this was an expedition... amongst seemingly pitch blackness. This time with all our Parkas zipped right up again. Walking as if subterranean periscopes. Single file we proceeded in trepidation. Wide eyed with our torches flashing. As was the moon occasionally visibly through the canopy. Hushed and muffled, we each of us followed, like the river itself. Our mini trek through Borneo or Papua New Guinea jungles. With bats and other sinister wildlife prowling, lurking hidden, concealed within nooks and caves, angry bears, snorting boars or even white fanged wolves. One of the teachers even tried to enhance the drama, by furtively hiding in the woods. Sneaking about nearby, spooking us by making strange owlish sounds! What was that? Listen – too whit too woo! There it was again. Until finally we reached the swinging rope bridge festooned over the Devils gorge. With red eyed trolls and rams horns fleeting deep within the dank cavernous abyss. We traversed, and returned safely back to camp for a ghostly story before slumber.

Later in the week, on gay still day we all hiked up the mountain. First one to the summit wins a pound! A pound of spuds it turned out. There were further lessons on geology – rocks! Something I never considered previously exempt of course merely for chucking. We also learned of early ancient settlers, farming folk, trees. I recollect garnering hazel nuts – real nuts and unsalted to boot. On another wet day all the kids watched a movie in the mess hall, about this wistful looking boy and his horse, set in Dartmoor or Yorkshire or some other such bleak windswept moor? Not forgetting to mention playing lots of football. In the early damp evenings beneath the dormitory eaves – 60 seconds, do kids still play that? One clear day we all rambled wearily to this little village of stone built cottages, its single room school and its handful of scholars. Walking along the narrow country lanes, the occasional bleating of sheep grazing upon the hillside and the ridge of old King Offa's Dyke stretching upon the horizon. One of the teachers mentioned Lester Piggott; maybe he'd had a flutter and Lester had just won the Derby riding Nijinsky? Lester Piggott I' heard of him and felt confident in my knowledge. A cultural icon such as Morecambe and Wise or Terry Wogan. The week triumphantly concluded with a visit to the Roman town of Chester. Built when centurions such as Charlton Heston governed Britain. We were then allowed further free recreational time from our living history lessons. So we all went shopping at Woolworths for presents. At last I got to spend all my secret 50p pieces. Before returning home to tell the tales!

Lately, these days I often sit outside the Harp Inn enjoying an ale and looking across the River Dee marshes to the Welsh Hills and Moel Famau yonder outlined in pastel. Often cycling across to Loggerheads passing by Colomendy once more still nestled amongst those expletives; sonorously just like Corylus avellana. Around hedge lined B roads and to Cilcain again – tu whit tu whoo – listen, can you hear it too?

In retrospect consider last summer

death in life three wishes to live longer

may have been hotter should have burnt brighter

but for the wind and the blasted showers

finally however the sun shone through

cooler beneath vines and ivy flowers

colluded till hazel became my hue

then to crack this shell and devour whit fruit

the nut of wisdom a small colloquy

to boot, life in death still as winters chill

a prismatic branch of colliding light

to wait a chance merely ingenuous

owls motionless call ever divining

hush... repose are the wings of a sonnet

this spinning wheel turns ever faster

till deep winter lays its plumage of snow

beware Robin red breast the days are brief

Tylluan screeches dusk then quietly swoops

unseen unheard the bloody thirteenth month

of sleeping mice and childhoods future

waxing awareness approaches dawn

falling catkins brushed golden as hair

too drink of the dew and feast on manna

for Apollo the lark hovers a hymn

heather bells echo with playground laughter

within nightfall she haunts luminous still

on tomb stones owls perched lucid alert

cadaverous desires tu whit and tu woo

serene Ishtar exalting beguiles

the mind awoken from her white pillow

when ruddy cock crows under mistletoe

is it beauty did the truth sound hollow?

this talash chorus my talisman theme

sloe barb wire berries your Nemesis seal

did the cuckoo grasp her Artemis hand?

mystery revealed mere dark taboo

Hermes turn into a shattering blow!

as with the lark flying high I roamed

silent fate multiplied thrice fore told

the waning moon winnows thru graveyards yew

cask of oak tenanted secure the brew

when iron latch falls white dove to renew

We may have little
control over the people
but we love them still

and how we *love them*?
we may only influence this
with all our loving

Where love is outlawed; all explained!
mysterious when romance removed -
then give magic the opportunity;
for the numinous may well exist to
become sentient and supernatural!
within that haunting limitless space
adrift and alone a boundless wildness
stalked by your fears acute the senses
pitch dark within the noise of their desires
awareness praised and all thoughts profound!
inhabiting your dreams the moonless night
all is affecting each rustle meaning
laughter your enemy smiling a foe
who is after you! Will you ever know?

Where, preparation meets potential -

I make this happen - moving the through the gears...

money an aphrodisiac... but not

at the fulcrum of my needs and desires

that will be you and you are who I want

this is my one intent - no reversal:

singularly driven with you at the wheel

so cocooned by that intimacy...

how fast will I be driven and how smooth

will your driving be... taking me with you

over these: more littered winter fragments:

the highways of fleeting intimations,

yet personal, acquiescent - speeding

through the cultural landscape of our minds

Ever wishful thinking if all were free

as the springs humming nostalgic breezy

golden the proverbs wild flower meadow

growing where this the spirit flourished

sensually poetic feelings nourished

contained by such like hedgerow sonnets

careless for ever never there will stir

soothing as the futures rich damson wine

bright the sunshine our horizons as clear

lolling around as an unkempt straggler

nobodies bother not once bothered

for I have this dignity that I can be

a person consumed by all that is free

responsible for all I can hear and see

Fresh! inhaling the sweet uplifting tang

charmed in his elementary best

green Donegal tweed cap with flecks of blue

donned was he as he swanned about

his pantaloons braced only he how

he knew and still how he knows he recalls

to whistle with glee for his old country

his home and his will ever present for

ever be he for this and for thee

his sustenance breathed he considers

the things most often ignored and cut

at the knees such like and such reveries

known as the kept and manicured fields

Sniff! fresh as those flecks of evening's bluebells

Don't attach too much significance
upon this dull wretched experience
it will pass like this bad cold or fever
the sun will shine and eventually
once again - the beaches are full of them!
those cuties there bodies all so ripped
sleeping off hangovers and bleaching hair
as for me preferably this hot toddy!
the miserable and gloomy day lives
prolonging the inevitability!
this winter this time and in the new year
similarly to last year more moaning
packed out trains and no room available
read! waves shucking over vacant pebble

Yr Wyddfa

Walking knows winters melting snow

feels great to be a nobody

even better just to be

I'm a working class project

this my work in action

refusing to be held back

not saying I aspire at

becoming something other

than who I am and

the work I excel at

if that be this or that

will be the work

that carries me on and on

"it is so... this instant when I see you:

I look at you and once more as ever;

want you and only you (there's no one else)

but nobody affects me as such; has

this hold on me; in the way that you act

offer your attraction this desire

for those crepuscular shadowed thighs

(telling me) relaxed and savouring her red wine...

"I do realise your attention;

you have indeed expressed yourself to me"

clearly honestly naked "I will (I want to) ...

but I need to be involved; I need commitment,

I demand and expect fidelity" spanning continents...

so will you now keep me and satisfy me –

(within me and all my needs)

#winter #fragments augmented parts

fully #involved #liman_maria #penrodpooch8

Two 2 know.

... with the Venus tide of her delta low,

stakes are high, the woman relaxed...

modo irreplaceably her;

she can almost touch

to taste the salty tang

taking "shape with my thoughts" tongue

for her filling estuary above

a wispy crepuscular spiritual

sky below sea and sandy beach

bathing heat pulsating

fresh bivalves... oysters waiting to be...

evening time labial

"taking shape with her thoughts"

Fragmented pieces: augmented parts

ամբողջ սրտով

Over scrubby heath jump in the puddles!

through prickly fields betwixt brooding sky's

and sometimes facing into driving rain

but more from stingin' nettles and scratchin' thorns

to feel the beating drum we march and shape

this link so arm in arm we form a chain

for us to hear or play the fiddle and

since all is long and at the end there is

a spoon for stirrin' and is rousing so

the fiddle plays a reel and we are dancin'

to its tune and it is reeling to and fro

so we can have a right good knees up!

Comment : С легким паром Какие планы после душа?

I'm frustrated! Frustrated in hell! All seems macabre – grotesque - sinister even! You see it's all this modernity! These new-fangled appliances! Fancy devices with their cameras you just point and shoot! After all how difficult could it be... maybe it's me simply becoming lucid! You understand I have this fantasy... I often dreamt of being a professional photographer (for all the major brands!) Due to the popularity of pictures these days I now view on Instagram I reckon I'd like to resume my passion and get back on to it! Dreaming... therefore I am now making a serious proposition: we have been following (hounding!) you Maria and your posts for a while now and I always want more Masha! I confess! Some may well regard this an obsession! And I agree! Your posts continually excite me along with your selfies...

(I'm thinking of the one of you in front of your mirror and the swish of your long dark whispering hair) you seem... and are communicating... saying something in Russian, then blowing (me) a kiss and moving your body only slightly wearing lingerie. Do you recall the one? I've watched this more times than I can count! So why not? What do you think? ... I suppose you may well be pre-empting this letter (a private modelling show perhaps?). However I wish to continue with this and more than just out of personal interest. To find out how you do it without an audience and for your followers? What say Masha? Photography! Pah! Just point and shoot (with or without processing)? Freeze framed! Celluloid! Stoop click!

Comment: above the steep... #liman-maria - fluorescent bikini post!

Сделай так, чтобы Я улыбнулась

Above the sea silence

Above the steep above the wave

Two evening stars

Two roads two destinies

And one of them is calling

Through the waves at sunrise

Here again the soul of the chansonchik wanted to sit on the shore and wait

(and the other is listening intently waiting still watching the waves crash upon my own distant shore expecting and needing your eastern soul - consumed within eternal space) some may say the subconscious self should be awakened! ... and its now 3am and I can't sleep and I've been thinking and contemplating matters and I'd like to start writing again to see where this takes me and it's raining outside and the fine sonority of falling rain with its suggestive and stimulating qualities... rain absorbing sensory as are you Maria... so could a novice, a learner, a debutante photographer work with you? Or am I really considering painting you? So being my subject my confidant possibly; expressive through art and similarly creating my-self breathing alive subjectively; a distant possibility or an impossibly but expansive and suggestive dream? (A further Endymion dream?) I repeat merely a novice photographer involved with you and driven by you as an experienced model with you deciding upon the situation, the style, the theme acting upon your guidance, with you directing and instructing me as to your aim, desires, wishes, needs... suggestively (lust Maria metaphysics once more)

Comment: Furthermore within the sphere of symbolism - for example... the erotic effect of your desired portrait! Click! This is how I dream of operating but also through words which in turn evoke or induce actions in the form of a response from the observer. In my case the viewer of your posts - consequently the pictures I would like to capture you there in... so as I write this I'm still and listening to the rain falling and now the rain has stopped... beating down...

Comment: Я планирую в будущем выпустить свою куклу   Я думаю она будет выглядеть именно так Осталось только определиться с размером Главное не отдавать ее китайским производителям

Between a model and the photographer should there develop a creative dialogue within the photographic session? I'm thinking verbally, laterally, developing a further connection. So tell me - do you look into the camera and project your own desires? Captivate entice, project (metaphysically Maria surely a further dream?). Through your look, your expression? Certainly this is as moving... look into this concave lens Maria searchingly more than a passing glance intensely your expression solely enhancing the physical self - click! Prompt encourage now reveal Maria this affect snap! your desire again click capture (envelope us) Your portrait, style of, wearing a black dress coffee snow maiden serene as the evening develops tempted so wandering through solid air scenic the springs elixir of life immediate and vibrant the crisp tasting apple crunch devour to savour... (Tranquil and simpler than solely using the expressive nature of one's physical self) in order to inform affect arouse desire upon me (no longer for your followers) Maria... thinking clearly (I need you to keep) these thoughts of ours we enjoyed as well versed and in control...

the galloping of spring an intoxicating thrill

of chase and explosion all change as ever will

summers charming story yet written to keep

dreaming pastoral scenes before darkness to sleep

Comment: pearls I wish to give you and shovel my ashes into a wheelbarrow!

Convex Concorde converse with me Maria modelling I presume is your chosen profession your career path basically and obviously however further more Maria aesthetically show me – snap! Request: is it frustrating working with many photographers? Personally you see I could be seen as a failed painter of sorts similarly Maria I find the artificial interface the hinterland if you get my drift most infuriating; (reflective) but I still feel intellectually intrigued inquisitive and engaged to float again once more…

Could this be; that it is the medium who frustrates the artist or vice versa?

Frustration; so let's imagine giving this a go; my taste leans towards cubism in painting; I find there exists movement and depth within stillness; similarly within sculpture I also look for movement; once again I feel this invokes an impression of movement by essentially a solid object. The work of art itself. If you are still following... how could I within you project movement and again for your numerous followers? Could I alone take you, invoke, project your sexual desires upon this audience? And under what circumstance and through which situation would you like to explore this enterprise? If indeed I can tempt you! Snap! Movement! Click once more I'm thinking of and considering, corresponding within a further art form. Art! Click! Hold... once more - again art exists within movement but paradoxically arrests, slows down and then - freeze frame movement in an instant! Snap! So the picture for me is not really the end result Maria? For you Maria these augmented parts... (still as time stalled, ceased to matter... apprehensive then once more time stalls; to fall further soft as lace falling, offering your once censored rose coloured nipples - now revealed to me – (to be my own) to need... my own apprehension also subtle; delicate as falling lace touching caressing... this my own personally; scented pink rose bud held as tentatively; searching... until the moment; the instant when - time springs free - manoeuvres grey matter transposing this upon you - my own white horse - once more moving mine into yours... the mysterious darkness within my approaching, probing awareness - this being infused now intimate...soon).

Comment: Consider subjective reality: situation, context, symbolism amongst, existence, a sense of place! Click... desire through movement. Snap! Experience this whilst modelling! Click! (I'm thinking of asking you a direct question) would you f*** me during a session of photography? (You know I didn't really say that?) Our lips are now sealed and yours Maria in response? Widen aperture – click! Now beguiled by your Persian hazel coloured eyes - click! Mysterious Maria – therefore kiss... me - clicked! To exist and become involved – unbridled Gothic monochromatic passion (realised!) Click! So continue to take me through an uninhibited session of photography Maria (a real life movie perhaps?) Obviously we understand and we agree to record such a session?

A lucky black cat - number 7 the surprise all boxed off... what does Maria Liman now wish to project upon my conscious desires? Through my point and shoot camera? Possibly giving an impression of movement - sound – vision - snap! What now springs to my mind? Click again immediately between us Maria! Snap selfie! If you told me and I wrote this down verbatim in black and white reading between the lines - would you then feel exposed? Or completely comfortable? Naked once more informing me giving me your immediate thoughts (I'm now wanting and needing to reach out and touch you) again would you now allow me both as novice photographer and inexperienced subject tell me how (so that we both feel simultaneously aroused) pleasure ecstasy may I now take absorb further sensations, details, within context (mutual symbiosis... telepathy!) Further suggestion - widen aperture - Click! This is now your black nights advance, approach, impress upon me inform me with your lips in your native tongue... Click click click (Unambiguously transpose then contemplate) connection again transform and then realise. Snap! Translate this into Russian - it has stopped raining and we wish to exist within the darkness to find our objective selves (ты будешь трахать меня Мария) - I never once spoke... this I am certain of my lips where sealed therefore surely silence (whisper... start) beginning I'd like to make love to you Maria (is love a broken and fragmented colour?)... Your narrative arc allows this Kandinsky rainbow - an Aesculapius aura! This page turns...

follow the curve of this narrative arc;

sub consciousness; shadows over chequered squares...

anticipation of my black Queen

to move aside her protecting knight;

authentic reasoning, these cadences;

strategic influencing of rhythm -

direct to Maria's page -

for pure Kandinsky colour

translated into Russian form...

vouchsafe this 3am concupiscence... cameleer trains lightly travel upon gabled windows to oracle shrines the hunting moon blinks and your feline eye stirs silhouette fir... darkling pupils ken then raven cloaked consciousness rotating dancer turns the minstrels spear to swim mid starlit temples...

amongst Cedar groves we understood

the role as the goat-herds alive and well

Artemis then now my deity to-be once again

a blue lotus flower in her fertile womb...

descriptive figuratively! Am I now skating on thin ice? Think of the implications! Such endeavours could they realistically be conceived and then perceived (misinterpreted maybe as dangerous) risk taking; foolhardy perhaps? Why? So consider briefly our own personal morals? Failing that; are those same morals now becoming obsolete? Now! It is starting to rain, memory persists once more I am now listening (and feeling a Tramontane breeze) to the wind outside express the breeze whispers, listen Maria did you hear? Thoughts now alive and healing will they change our minds regarding such bold propositions? Connection; in tune with the weather? - do you now think that morals should be thoroughly ignored and or completely removed from this situation? Say yes! Please instantly! Click click - clicked - wow let's go for it! Snap! Snapped! Once again this our situation: outside or inside? Landscape: problems - light, temperature etc. Inside: control of light and temperature - darkness, shade. Further physical considerations now influenced, affecting this our (sensual) mood? Distance – focus click! The tone and the feeling captured – snap! Lost the connection? Then breathe in to then taste - click! Clicked! I will hold you... so caress this memory; the rain has now ceased and there exists silence outside amongst the silhouetted trees gloaming nuanced framed silver twilight as such an owl calls... (Screeches – swoops!) – click! An echo forms... what next - next? The future, future – I am now thinking of touch but something prevents me (what made me think of touch?) A loss of feeling? Anxious? I am now thinking of saying something nice; but perhaps this keeps me guarded? Shade! Back to movement to now express desire. Don't think! Inhale let yourself feel. Now imagine and tell me what came into our minds? You first! I await the response do recall this sensation then now tell me the first thing you thought of! Snap! Let's connect once more... now feel the soft melodic cadences - the trans-migration of snow (ձյուն աղջիկը) that drifts and floats way out beyond the hinterland and over falling amongst the Caucus mountains ranging Maria... a burning militia a Cossack wild and free...

so once more the moment hangs like swans wings beating - Leda (you

be) streams of consciousness fluid curving back through antiquity -

mythology and to return inundating your estuary amongst an Armenia

diaspora... wow click click clicked! Reality briefly captured again!

a white swan creaming... Leda my own trans-mission

over miniature storms and kingdoms...

each night I travel east and we meet... I

then rise greeting you as the morning sun...

Comment: Цвет настроения синий Синий иней, синей иней... Уууу! Уууу-гу... Синие люди Аватары

an age of flight over flower meadows

the evergreen calendar lights the wik

of the golden five pointed secret

shining eyes of black night watching

pleasures of blood lust crimson stained

within Ishtar able bronzed

consequently! Action scene one turn over the page. I have noticed you feel comfortable being naked. But still I feel your selfies are more expressive of serendipitous pleasure to me. Why? Or why do I consistently hold this thought. Are suggestive thoughts attracted when combined, harmonious, visionary, natural, and responsive again when naked and real! Click click click!

Comment: No? Yes? (I wish to commit to you completely and <u>от всего сердца</u>) momentarily again I'm now thinking of you smiling with flowing hair and I'm now moving inside you. When? Soon... Now speak to me in your native tongue truly I find this most revealing - most erotic. Would you dare to? Are we tempted? But you are now experienced and in full control of your own female sexuality - Click! But let us not think about controlling ourselves let us no longer think. Anymore Maria? Click! This is a proposal furthermore - act!

Comment: Have we now slept on this? And are you now therefore refreshed and comfortable? Yes? Keep your dreams a secret then... now let's commence with this photography session tonight! Clicked!

Один раз в год сады цветут

Весну любви один раз ждут

Всего один лишь только раз

Цветут сады в душе у нас

Один лишь раз   один лишь раз

when we realise the strength that keeps me wanting you

our understanding well my arms embracing us

as and when you decide and turn our page to read

see all was written with our souls and minds revealed

Comment: Доброе утро! Кто уже не спит? Москва, наверно ещё и не ложилась спать Из каких городов, мои любимые подписчики?

Comment: that spell you crafted and concocted is starting to have an effect on me! Spectral – supernatural – magic even! (Maybe I have been reading too much Mann or even Nabokov! lately!)

Then again... it is now early evening and still daylight grey and cloudy even a fool could forecast rain for its precipitous affect... let me think it through the rain will eventually stop falling so now let's enjoy the sonorous quality - anticipating pleasure, of feeling our way through the approaching pitch dark night rain free of anxiety within our own mutually perceived subconscious so therefore productive minds - blue – green and then black consciousness... above the steep two stars revealed...

Firebird suit.

A wise act to fathom aquiline streams…

and soar among many snow caped peaks

with savage faith in *tercel* folded wings

breach Arcadian iron boundaries…I

challenge Prospero dance *dance* on savage earth

let instinct rule motion yes heathen be

sensor constellations bristles silver firs

cast shaded thoughts in peaceful blue

Prospero *dance dance* in ritual symmetry

now instinct rules motion modo be!

….and listen once again the rites of spring

drifts the bassoon; your futures sublime memory…

absolute freedom sacrifice reigns supreme!

now rhythmic sound rains rain beats green again…

returning; welcome back relax now be seated by this fire and watch the flames listen to the crackle of burning wood (he really thinks... he could be! – be Mephistopheles!) Where was we? Where could we be? Situation, circumstance, contextualize along with me. Remember I am still a bit of an amateur but I've been doing some homework, learning to focus, zoom understand and grasp this opportunity – Maria your page and each post interest me on a number of levels... so let's play a further mind game: I once practised this whilst meditating... visualise this ancient ceramic pot I am describing as such; a most treasured piece - antique and Greek - a black amphora perfumed and sweet - now close your eyes – I'm smashing that pot to pieces! Listen! Keep them closed! Texture feel! The pot at this moment exists only in fragmented pieces within our imagined selves and is strewn about the floor with its contents spilt. Now open your eyes and gaze into the fires flames and imagine that very same vase once again whole (amongst the Caucus mountain range) now read the symbolism depicted upon that pot, its illustrations of dancing satyrs along with Dionysus offering 'them' well preserved wine - so would you now - fancy a glass of red wine? A bottle even to drink to share with me; these augmented pieces...

still as time stalled, ceased to matter;

apprehensive then once more time stalls to

fall further soft as lace; subtle as your

censored rose coloured nipples now

revealed to me - to be my own to

touch... my own apprehension also;

soft as lace falling touching caressing...

this my own personal soft scented pink

rose bud held as tentatively; presents...

until the moment when - time springs free

manoeuvres grey matter transposing this

upon you; my own white horse once more moves

mine into yours... the darkness within our

approaching infused intimacy

Comment: Тук-тук! Чем Вы занимаетесь?

Comment: Что лучше всего выпить перед сном, чтобы Ночь прошла незабываемо?

then silence… so Maria now listen to some music… its 4 in the morning the end of December

many peasants dance amongst the trees

Saturnalias festivities - click click!

clicked into place as ever

the she wolves' teeth concealed

Robin sings high amongst the holly leaves

Biddy bee lord of the hinged door swings

where wren and oak are one and open

to telepathy! a golden reign succeeds!

аватар - AvAtar

I found U within the Apple

so enticed by U - your estuary

of Venus beneath weeping willows U

are reading this poem we must exist

- when I breach over your seas and reads

                into AvAlon Maria

beneath a planet known as Saturn with

in a pentad we worship as colours

entwined like Adam and Eve in U

this Atom Explodes when in synergy

we become as one in sincerity

till our spirits explodes into a...

                sTAR!

Printed in Great Britain
by Amazon

42239624R00028